We All Go Traveling By

BUS
STOP

Written by **Sheena Roberts**   Illustrated by **Siobhan Bell**

Barefoot Books
Celebrating Art and Story

I spy with my little eye,
You can hear with your little ear,

A yellow school bus goes *beep-beep-beep.*

And we all go traveling by, bye-bye,
And we all go traveling by.

I spy with my little eye,
You can hear with your little ear,

A bright red truck goes *rumble-rumble-rumble.*

A yellow school bus goes *beep-beep-beep.*

And we all go traveling by, bye-bye,
And we all go traveling by.

I spy with my little eye,
You can hear with your little ear,

A long blue train goes *chuff-chuff-chuff*.

A bright red truck goes *rumble-rumble-rumble*.
A yellow school bus goes *beep-beep-beep*.

**And we all go traveling by, bye-bye,
And we all go traveling by.**

**I spy with my little eye,
You can hear with your little ear,**

A shiny pink bike goes *ring-ring-ring.*

A long blue train goes *chuff-chuff-chuff.*

A bright red truck goes *rumble-rumble-rumble*.

A yellow school bus goes *beep-beep-beep.*

**And we all go traveling by, bye-bye,
And we all go traveling by.**

I spy with my little eye,
You can hear with your little ear,

A little green boat goes *chug-a-lug-a-lug*.

A shiny pink bike goes *ring-ring-ring*.

A long blue train goes *chuff-chuff-chuff.*

A bright red truck goes *rumble-rumble-rumble.*

A yellow school bus goes *beep-beep-beep.*

**And we all go traveling by, bye-bye,
And we all go traveling by.**

I spy with my little eye,
You can hear with your little ear,

A big white plane goes *neeeeeeee-oww.*

A little green boat goes
chug-a-lug-a-lug.

A shiny pink bike goes *ring-ring-ring.*

A long blue train goes *chuff-chuff-chuff.*

A bright red truck goes *rumble-rumble-rumble.*

A yellow school bus goes *beep-beep-beep.*

**And we all go traveling by, bye-bye,
And we all go traveling by.**

I spy with my little eye,
You can hear with your little ear,

A fast orange car goes
vroom-vroom-vroom.

A big white plane goes
neeeeeeee-oww.

A little green boat goes *chug-a-lug-a-lug.*

A shiny pink bike goes *ring-ring-ring.*

A long blue train goes *chuff-chuff-chuff.*

A bright red truck goes *rumble-rumble-rumble.*

A yellow school bus goes *beep-beep-beep.*

**And we all go traveling by, bye-bye,
And we all go traveling by.**

**I spy with my little eye,
You can hear with your little ear,**

Two purple shoes go *tap-tap-tap*.

A fast orange car goes *vroom-vroom-vroom*.

A big white plane goes *neeeeeeee-oww*.

A little green boat goes *chug-a-lug-a-lug*.

A shiny pink bike goes *ring-ring-ring*.

A long blue train goes *chuff-chuff-chuff*.
A bright red truck goes *rumble-rumble-rumble*.
A yellow school bus goes *beep-beep-beep*.

**And we all go traveling by, bye-bye,
And we all go traveling by.**

I spy with my little eye,
You can hear with your little ear,

A loud silver bell goes
ding-a-ling-a-ling.

And we all start another school day,

hooray!

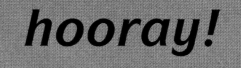

And we all start another school day!

Traveling By!

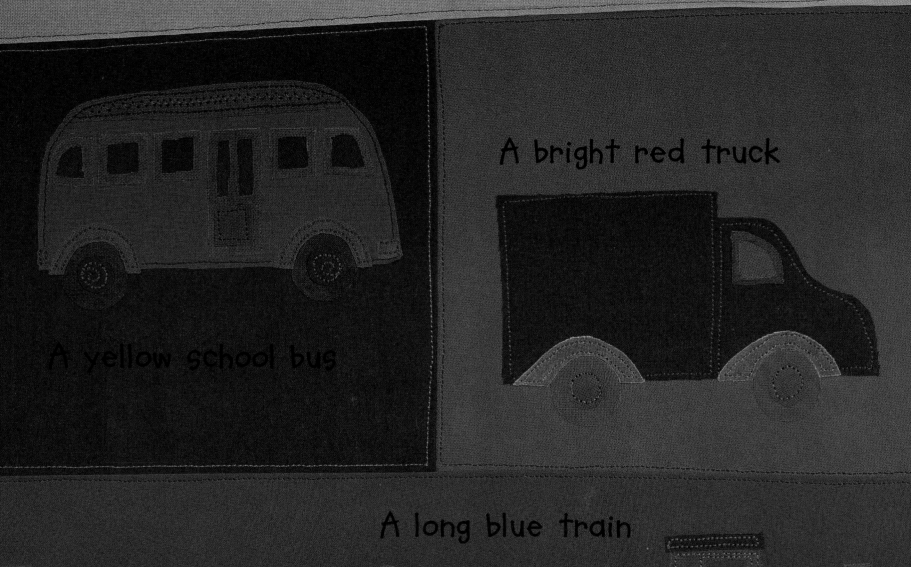

A yellow school bus

A bright red truck

A long blue train

A big white plane

A shiny pink bike

A fast orange car

A little green boat

Two purple shoes

For Charlie and Jake — S. R.

For Vini — S. B.

Barefoot Books
2067 Massachusetts Avenue, 5th Floor
Cambridge MA 02140

This book was typeset in Symbol and SoupBone
The illustrations were prepared using hand-dyed cotton sheets

Graphic design by Barefoot Books, Bath, England
Color separation by Bright Arts, Singapore
Printed and bound in Singapore by Tien Wah Press Pte Ltd

This book has been printed on 100% acid-free paper

1 3 5 7 9 8 6 4 2

Publisher Cataloging-in-Publication Data (U.S.)

Roberts, Sheena.
    We all go traveling by / written by Sheena Roberts ; illustrated by
Siobhan Bell. —1st ed.
[24] p. : col. ill. ;   cm.
Accompanied by musical compact disc.
Summary: A cumulative sing-song text takes children on a journey to
school, introducing them to many different modes of transportation,
sounds, colors, and adjectives.
ISBN 1-84148-168-8
1. Schools — Fiction — Juvenile literature. (1. Schools — Fiction.
2. Stories in rhyme.) I. Bell Siobhan. II. Title.
  [E] 21   PZ7.R6347We 2003

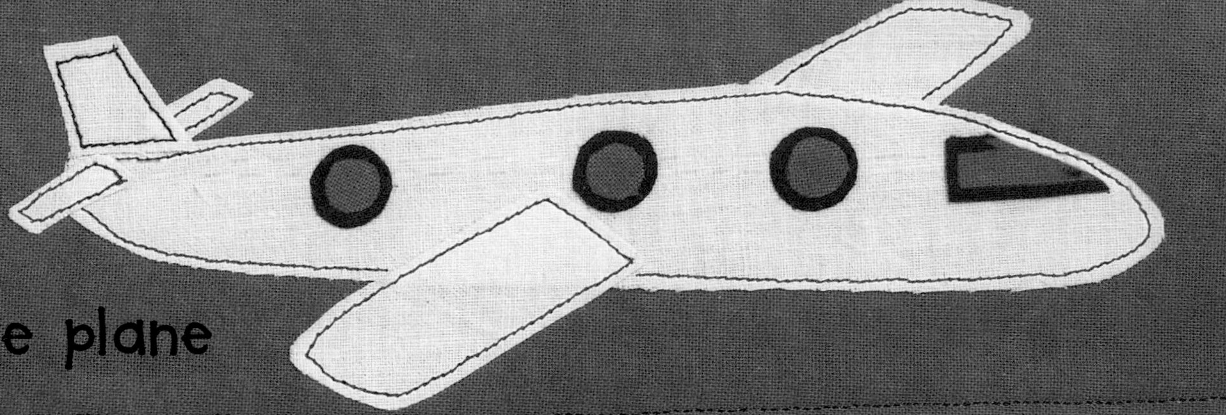

A big white plane

A shiny pink bike

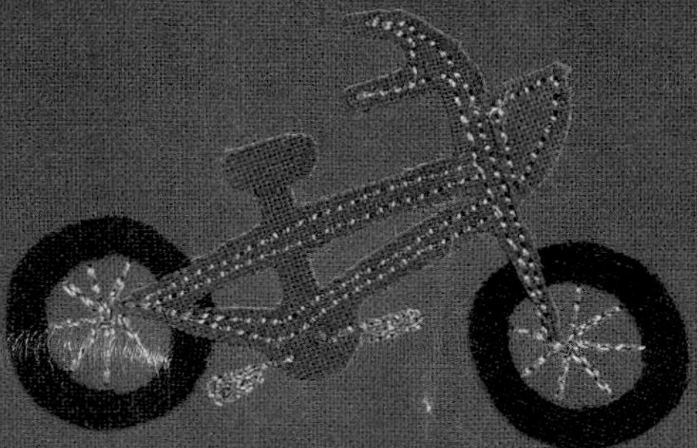

A fast orange car

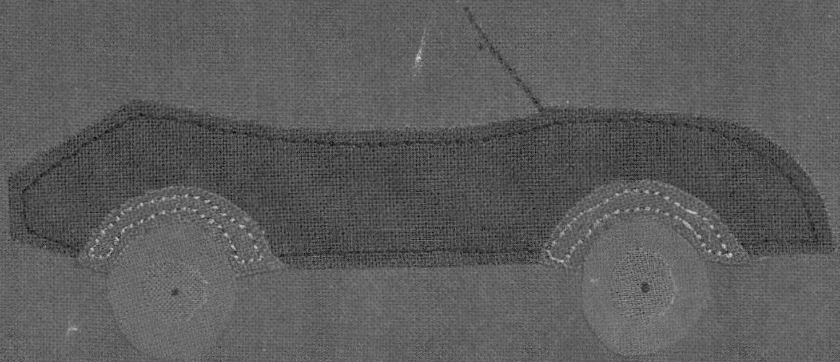

A little green boat

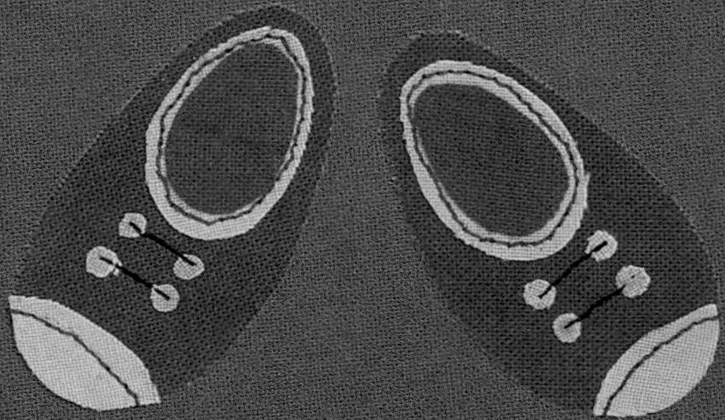

Two purple shoes

For Charlie and Jake — S. R.

For Vini — S. B.

Barefoot Books
2067 Massachusetts Avenue, 5ᵗʰ Floor
Cambridge MA 02140

This book was typeset in Symbol and SoupBone
The illustrations were prepared using hand-dyed cotton sheets

Graphic design by Barefoot Books, Bath, England
Color separation by Bright Arts, Singapore
Printed and bound in Singapore by Tien Wah Press Pte Ltd

This book has been printed on 100% acid-free paper

1 3 5 7 9 8 6 4 2

Publisher Cataloging-in-Publication Data (U.S.)

Roberts, Sheena.
    We all go traveling by / written by Sheena Roberts ; illustrated by
Siobhan Bell. —1st ed.
[24] p. : col. ill. ; cm.
Accompanied by musical compact disc.
Summary: A cumulative sing-song text takes children on a journey to
school, introducing them to many different modes of transportation,
sounds, colors, and adjectives.
ISBN 1-84148-168-8
1. Schools — Fiction — Juvenile literature. (1. Schools — Fiction.
2. Stories in rhyme.) I. Bell Siobhan. II. Title.
    [E] 21   PZ7.R6347We 2003

Barefoot Books
Celebrating Art and Story

At Barefoot Books, we celebrate art and story with books that open the hearts and minds of children from all walks of life, inspiring them to read deeper, search further, and explore their own creative gifts. Taking our inspiration from many different cultures, we focus on themes that encourage independence of spirit, enthusiasm for learning, and acceptance of other traditions. Thoughtfully prepared by writers, artists and storytellers from all over the world, our products combine the best of the present with the best of the past to educate our children as the caretakers of tomorrow.

www.barefootbooks.com